MALCOLM'S MARTIANS: EXPLORING MARS

Beneath the Surface: A Race Against Time

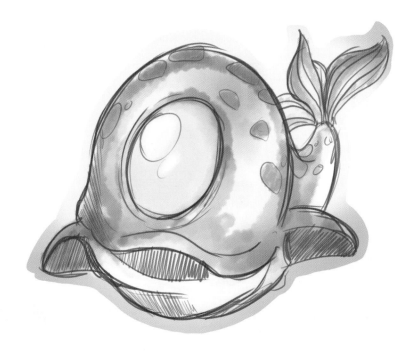

by Jason M. Burns

illustrated by Dustin Evans

TORCH GRAPHIC PRESS

Published in the United States of America by Cherry Lake Publishing Group
Ann Arbor, Michigan
www.cherrylakepublishing.com

Reading Adviser: Beth Walker Gambro, MS, Ed., Reading Consultant, Yorkville, IL

Book Designer: Book Buddy Media

Torch Graphic Press is an imprint of Cherry Lake Publishing Group.

Library of Congress Cataloging-in-Publication Data has been filed and is available at catalog.loc.gov

Cherry Lake Publishing Group would like to acknowledge the work of the Partnership for 21st Century Learning, a Network of Battelle for Kids. Please visit http://www.battelleforkids.org/networks/p21 for more information.

Printed in the United States of America
Corporate Graphics

TABLE OF CONTENTS

Mission log: August 22, 2055.

This morning Dad joked that I needed to have my swim trunks ready for today's exploration. I don't know what he has in store for us, but my friend, Daniela, can't wait to learn more about any potential water on Mars. I am excited too. If we are venturing away from land, it will give me a whole new type of Martian to draw. Fins and gills, here I come!

—Malcolm Thomas

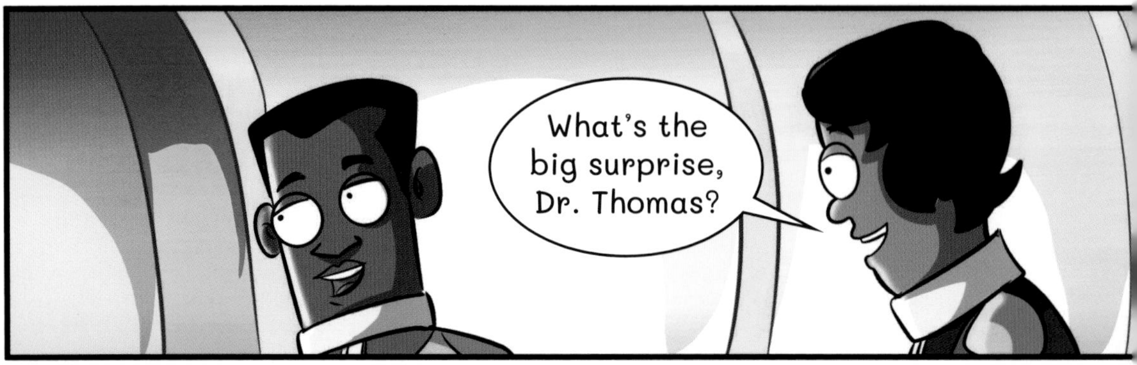
What's the big surprise, Dr. Thomas?

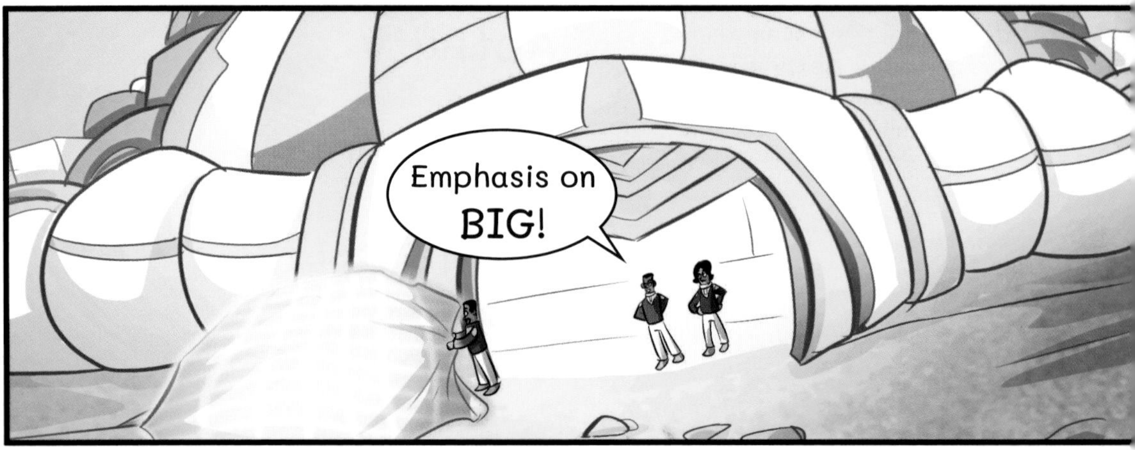
Emphasis on BIG!

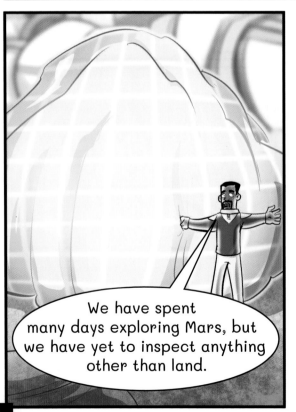

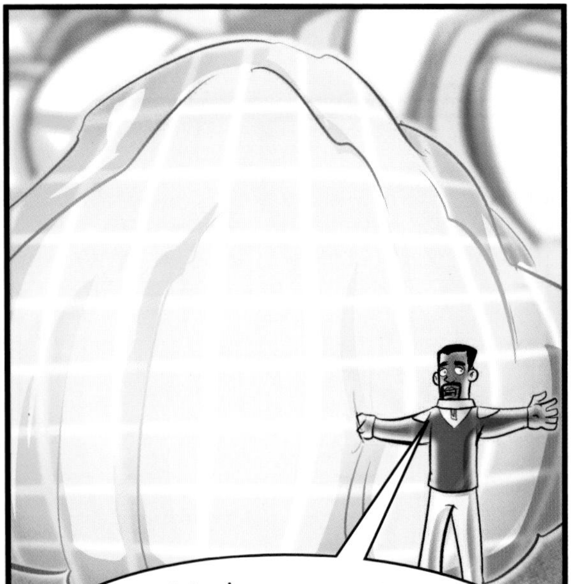
We have spent many days exploring Mars, but we have yet to inspect anything other than land.

MARS FACT

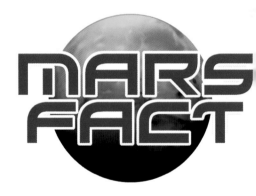

Mars is a terrestrial planet. That means the planet has a metallic c is made up of rock, and has a hard surface.

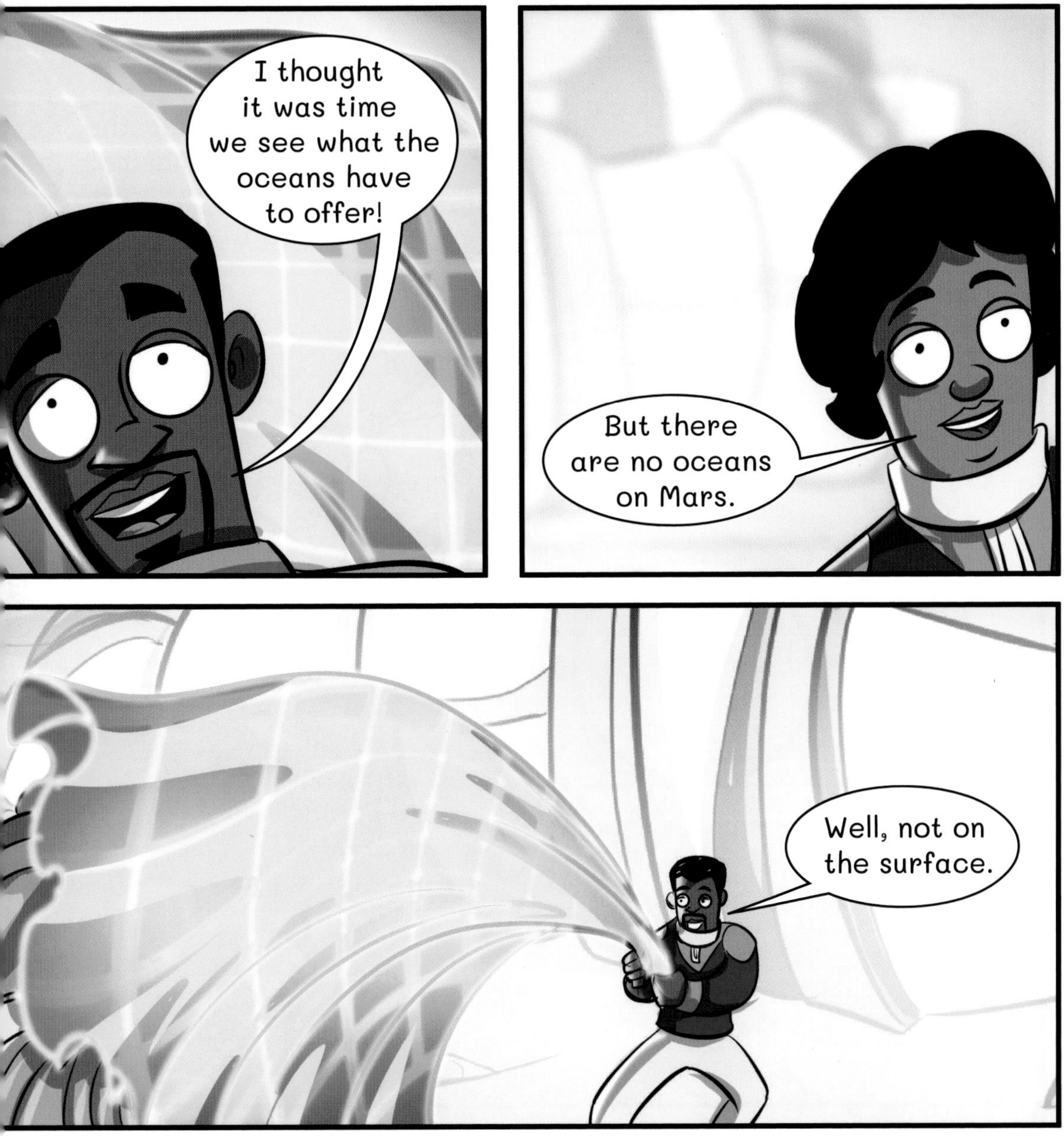
I thought it was time we see what the oceans have to offer!
But there are no oceans on Mars.
Well, not on the surface.

MARS FACT

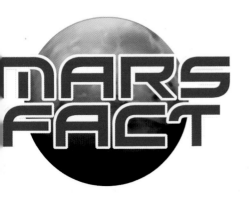

Researchers believe there are a number of underground bodies of water on Mars.

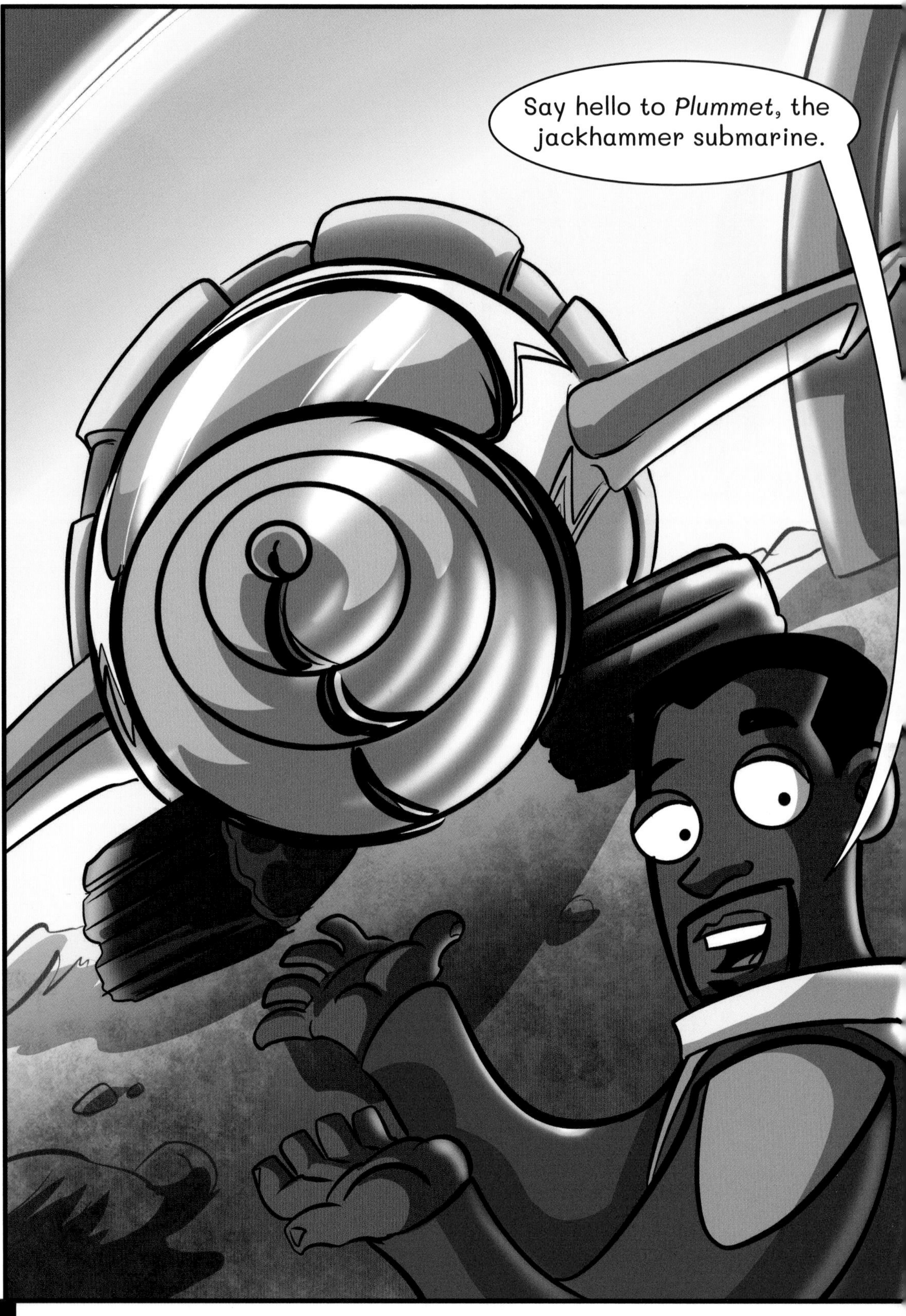
Say hello to *Plummet*, the jackhammer submarine.

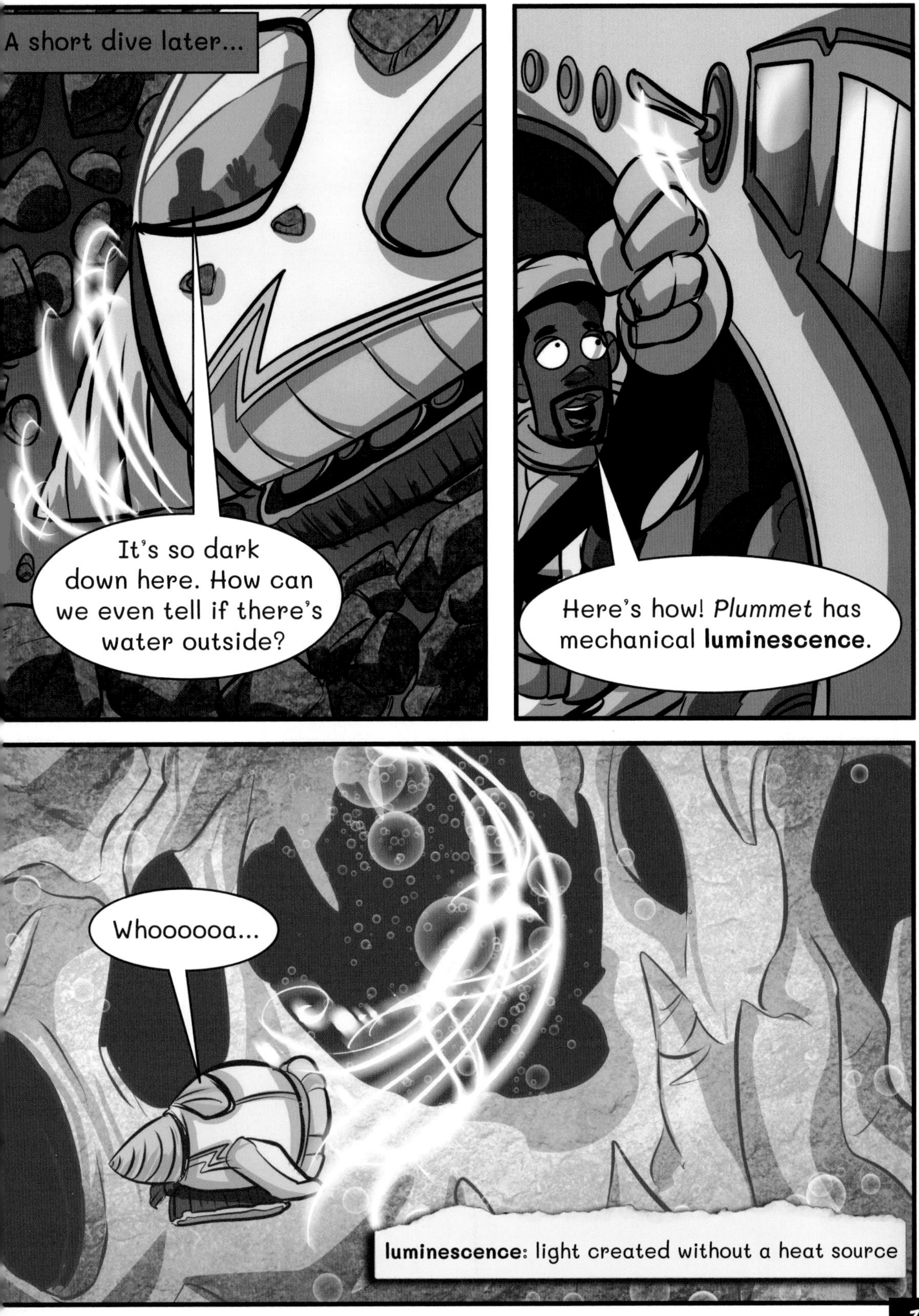
A short dive later...
It's so dark down here. How can we even tell if there's water outside?
Here's how! *Plummet* has mechanical **luminescence**.
Whoooooa...
luminescence: light created without a heat source

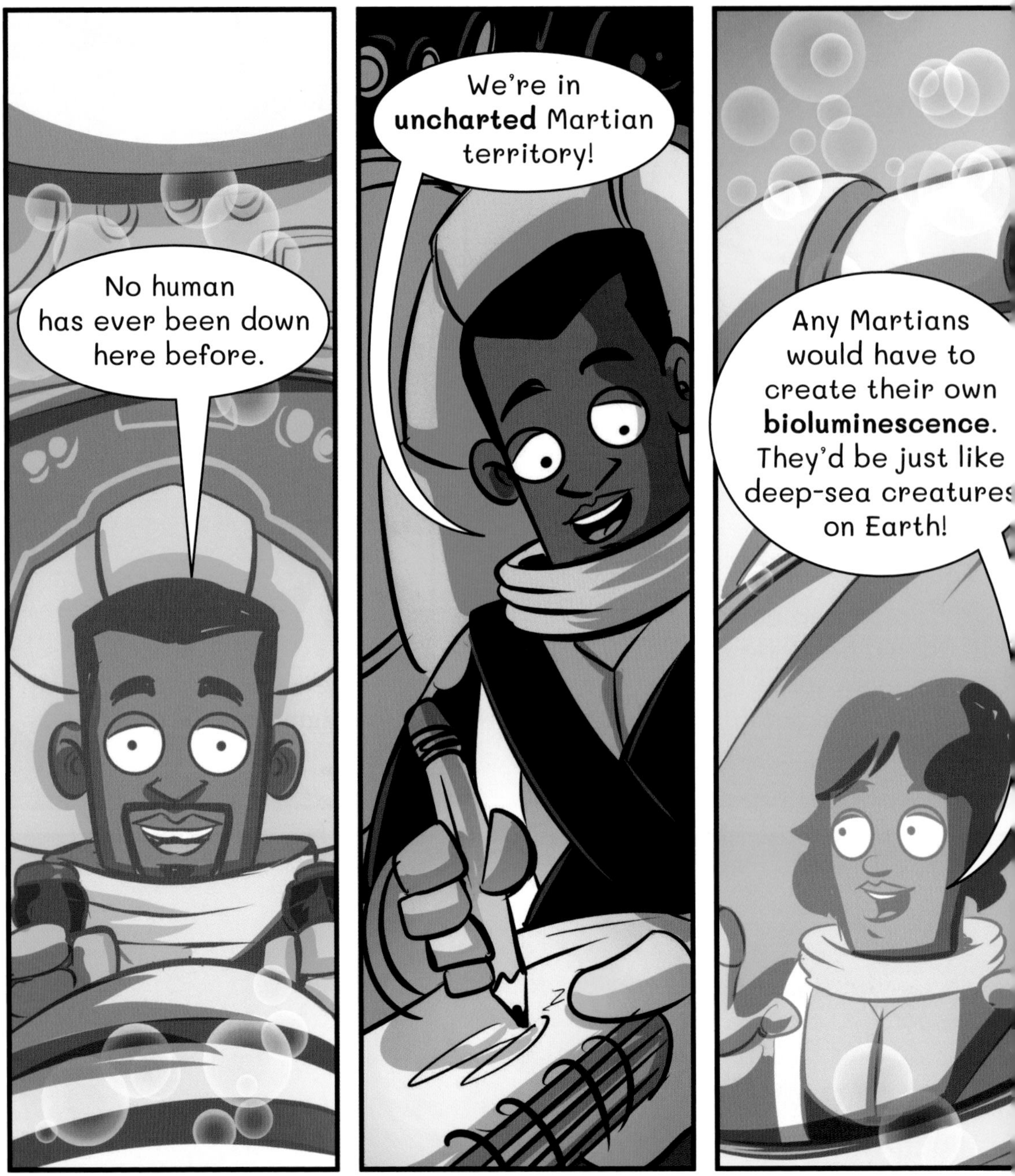
No human has ever been down here before.
We're in **uncharted** Martian territory!
Any Martians would have to create their own **bioluminescence**. They'd be just like deep-sea creature
on Earth!

SCIENCE FACT

Bioluminescent animals on Earth inclu
jellyfish, squid, and fireflies.

uncharted: not yet explored

bioluminescence: light created by a living organi

THE CASE FOR SPACE

Is there really water beneath the surface of Mars? Thanks to discoveries made by technology, researchers think there is. Let's dive in to some Mars water facts!

• The first underground body of water on Mars was discovered in 2018.

• In 2020, 3 additional bodies of water were also discovered.

• All 4 are considered to be saltwater lakes.

• The discovery was made using radar from *Mars Express*, the European Space Agency's spacecraft.

• The European Space Agency is Europe's version of the National Aeronautics and Space Administration (NASA).

• Scientists believe these underground bodies of water to be the remains of what were once vast Mars oceans.

• The lakes are located deep beneath the planet's south pole.

• They have been unfrozen due to the heat given off by the planet's core.

• These underground bodies of water have never been explored. There are still many unanswered questions about what they are and how they were formed.

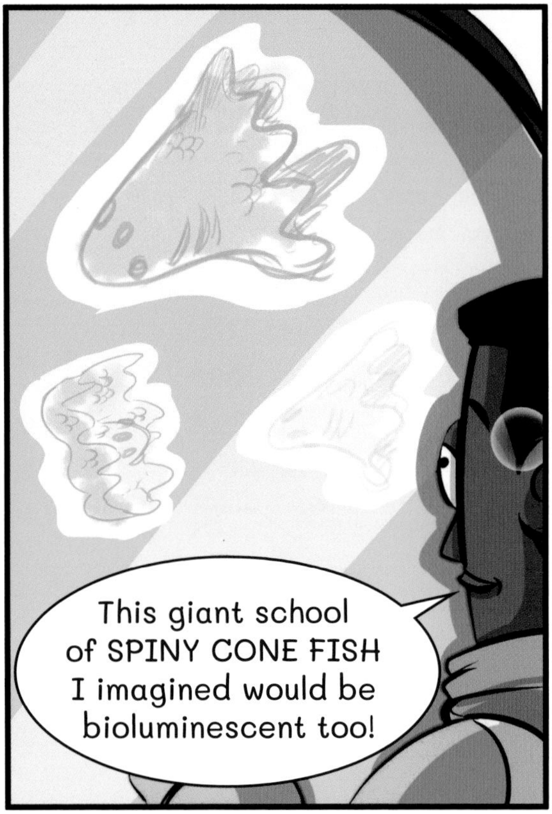
This giant school of SPINY CONE FISH I imagined would be bioluminescent too!

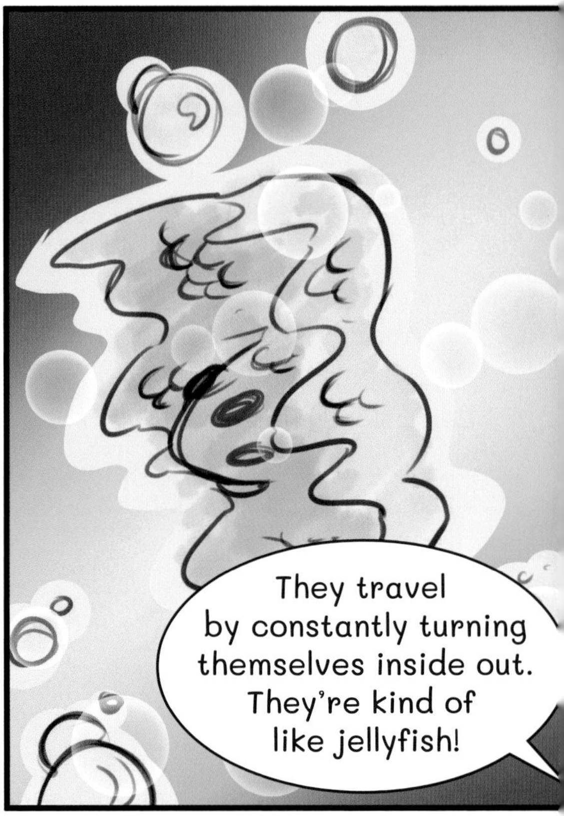
They travel by constantly turning themselves inside out. They're kind of like jellyfish!

SCIENCE FACT

Jellyfish don't have brains, hearts or blood.

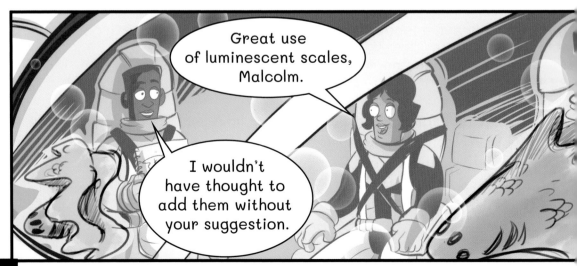

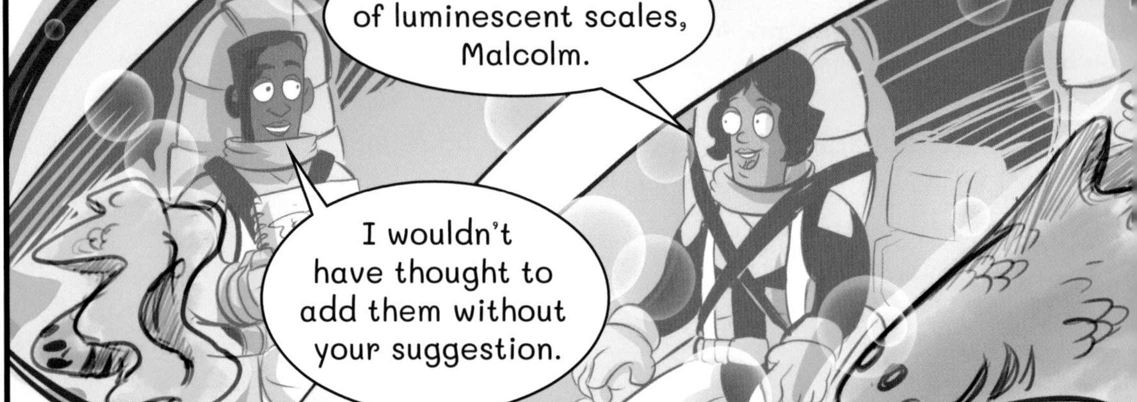
Great use of luminescent scales, Malcolm.
I wouldn't have thought to add them without your suggestion.

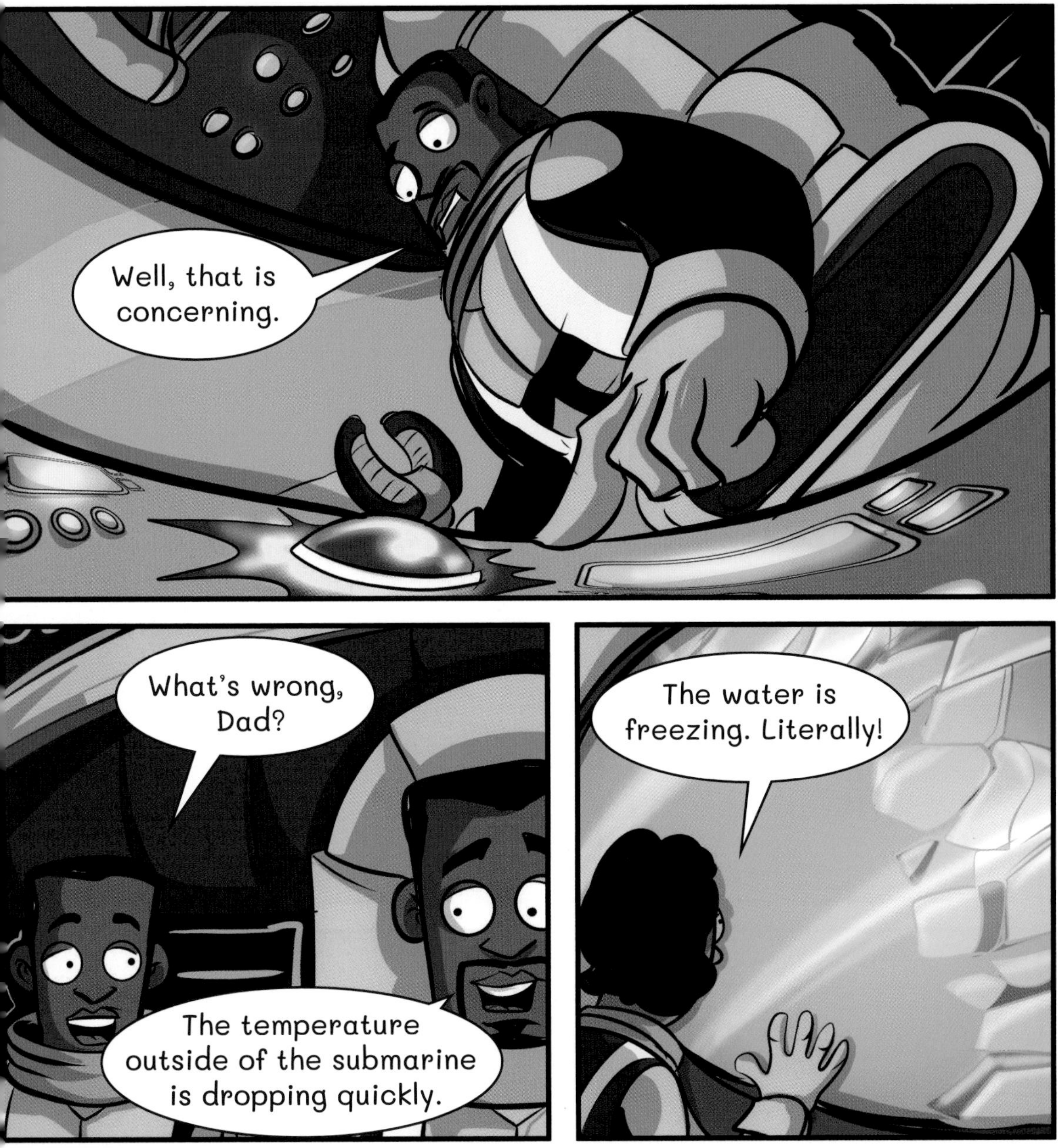
Well, that is concerning.
What's wrong, Dad?
The temperature outside of the submarine is dropping quickly.
The water is freezing. Literally!

MARS FACT

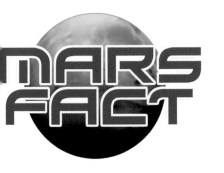

Mars is cold. The average temperature on Mars is about -80 degrees Fahrenheit (-60 degrees Celsius). By comparison, the average temperature on Earth is 59°F (15°C).

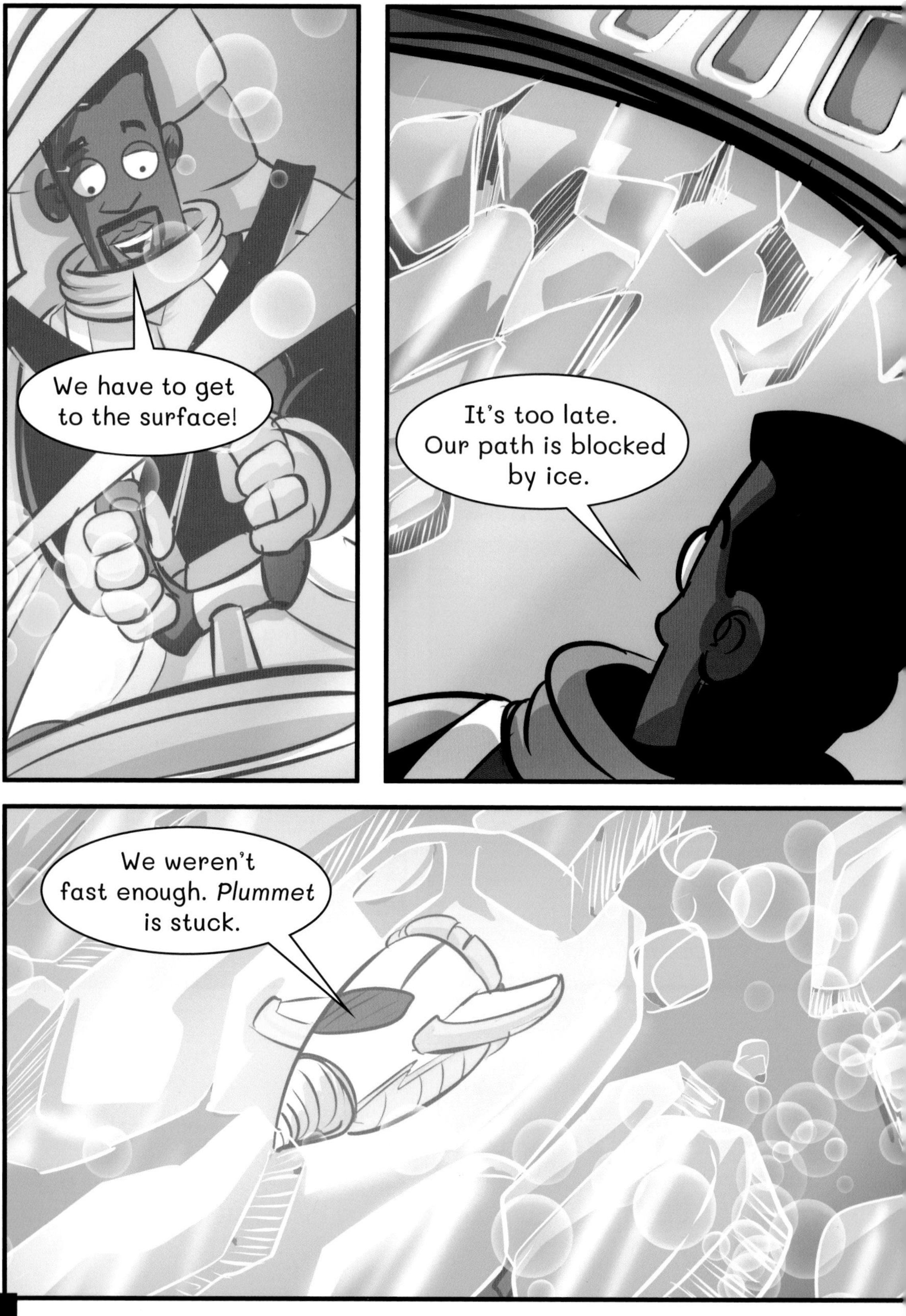
We have to get to the surface!
It's too late. Our path is blocked by ice.
We weren't fast enough. *Plummet* is stuck.

THE SCIENCE OF SCIENCE FICTION

The team is learning firsthand just how cold it can get on Mars. Extreme temperatures impact more than just humans. Everything gets cold, even machines. Let's take a look at how scientists protect the technology they send to the Red Planet, including rovers like *Perseverance*.

• Rovers will not operate as intended when in extreme temperatures.

• The main components scientists want to protect are the batteries, electronics, and the computer.

• Scientists use special heaters to protect those parts from the cold Mars temperatures.

• *Perseverance* was built with a thermostat-controlled heater that maintains a temperature of 45°F (7.2°C).

• The rover's body is called the Warm Electronics Box (WEB).

• Rover bodies are painted with gold coating to keep heat from escaping.

• Scientists also use a special kind of **insulation** called aerogel. Aerogel is nicknamed "solid smoke" because it is 99.8 percent air.

insulation: material used to keep heat from escaping

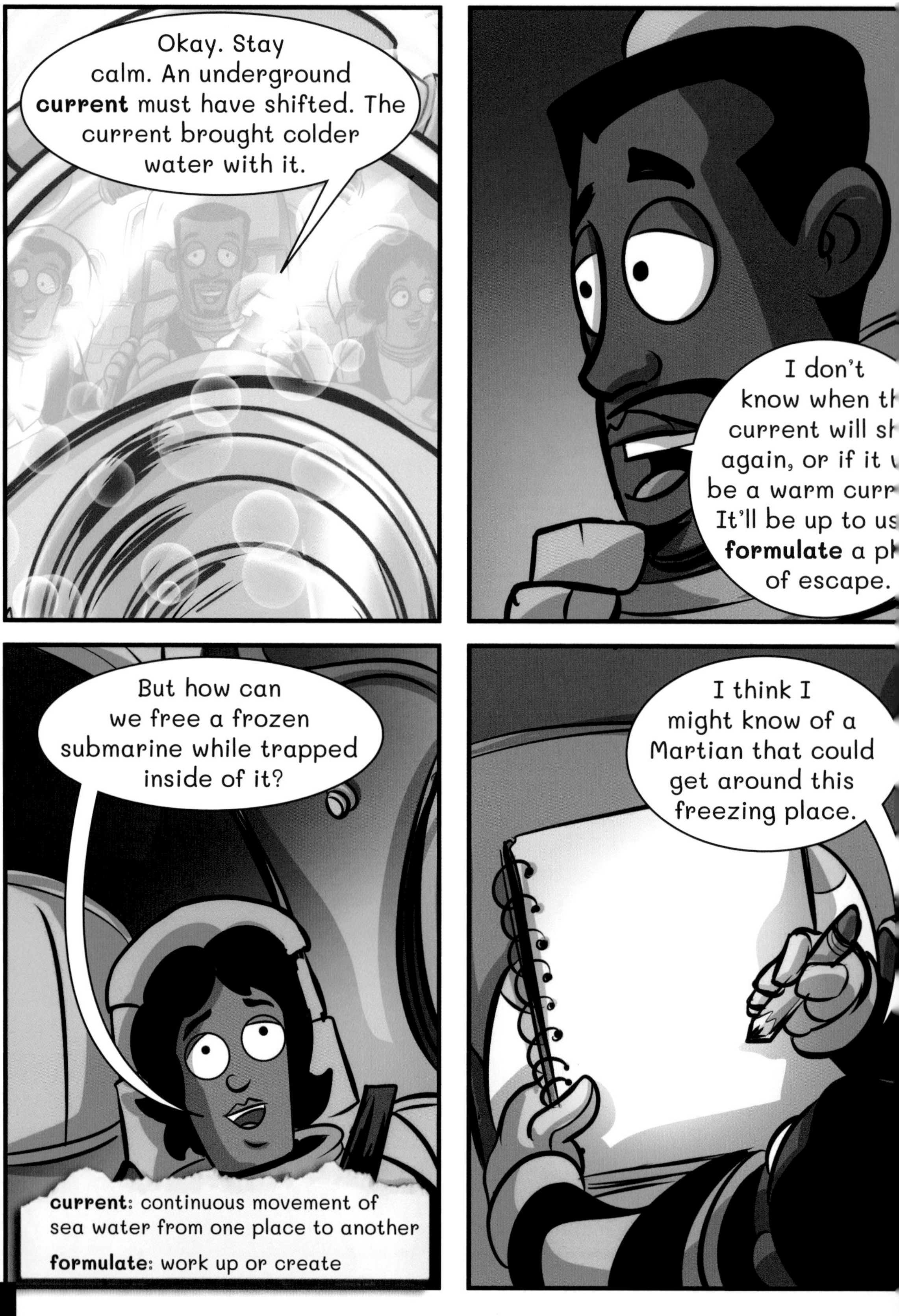
Okay. Stay calm. An underground **current** must have shifted. The current brought colder water with it.
I don't know when t current will s again, or if it be a warm curr It'll be up to u **formulate** a p of escape.
But how can we free a frozen submarine while trapped inside of it?
I think I might know of a Martian that could get around this freezing place.

current: continuous movement of sea water from one place to another

formulate: work up or create

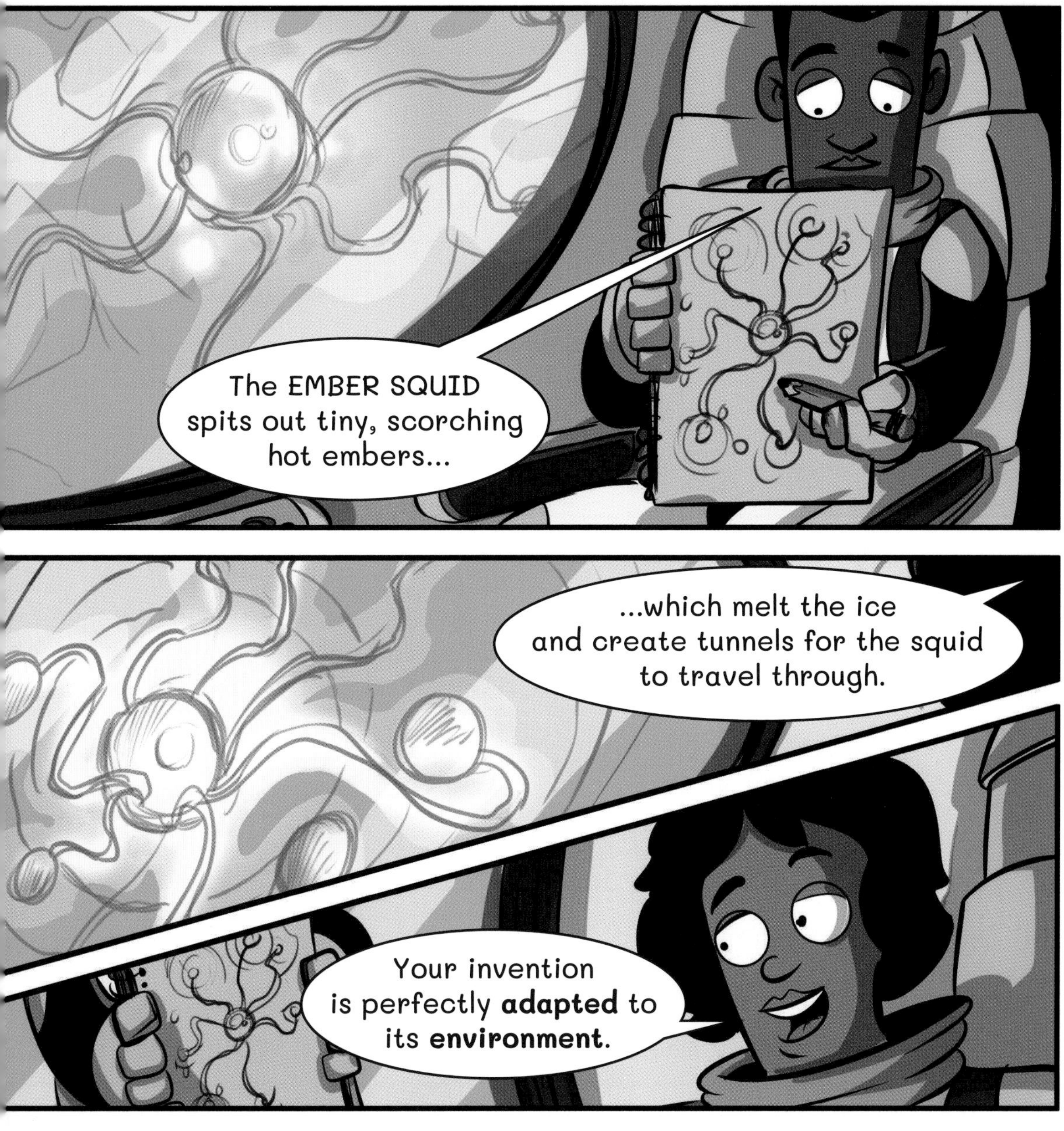
The EMBER SQUID spits out tiny, scorching hot embers...
...which melt the ice and create tunnels for the squid to travel through.
Your invention is perfectly **adapted** to its **environment**.

SCIENCE FACT

On Earth, a mammal perfectly adapted to the extreme cold is the arctic ground squirrel. Its brain can power down during hibernation. This protects its brain from the cold until it wakes up in the spring.

adapted: to become adjusted to new conditions

environment: the specific place where an animal lives

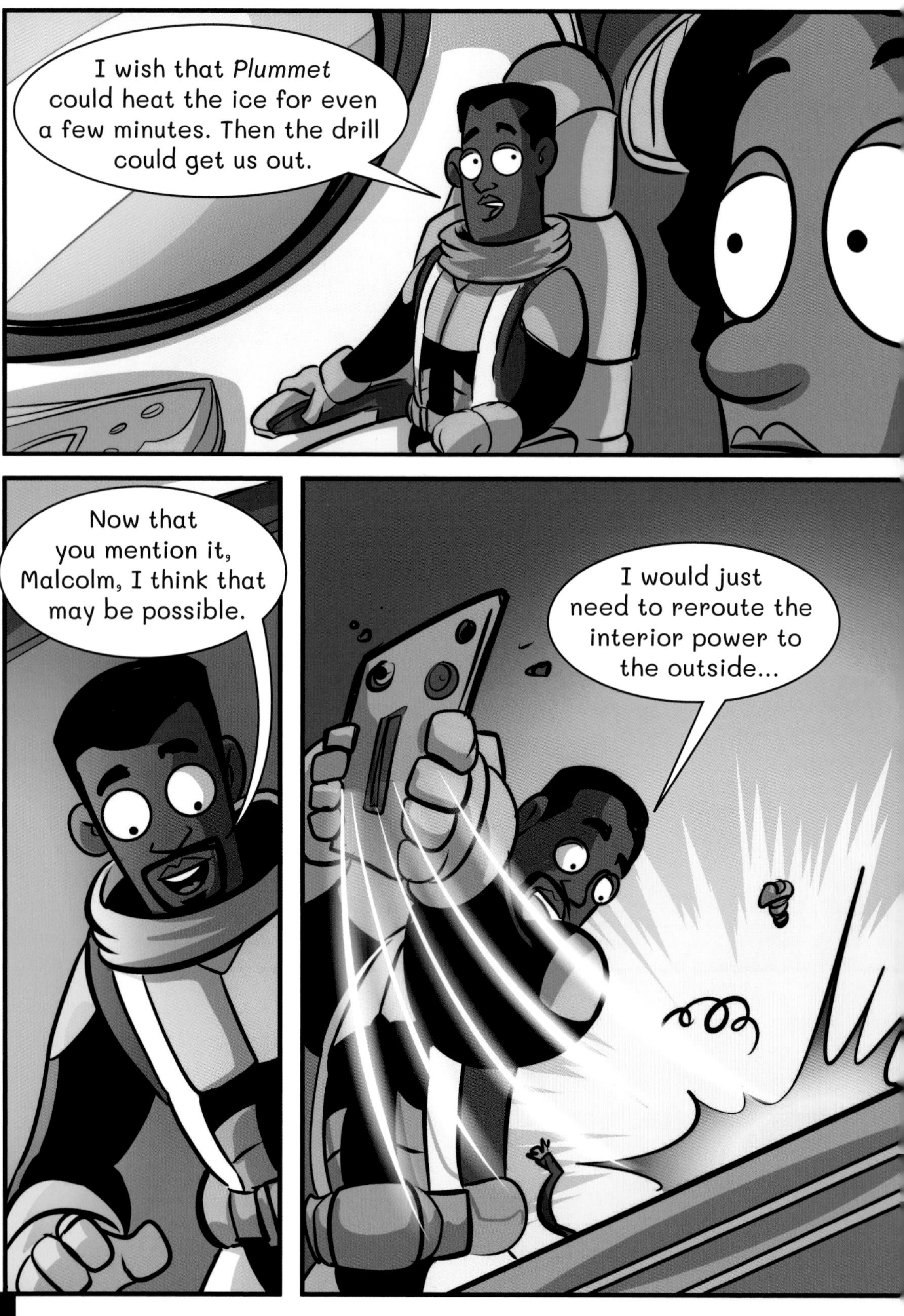
I wish that *Plummet* could heat the ice for even a few minutes. Then the drill could get us out.
Now that you mention it, Malcolm, I think that may be possible.
I would just need to reroute the interior power to the outside...

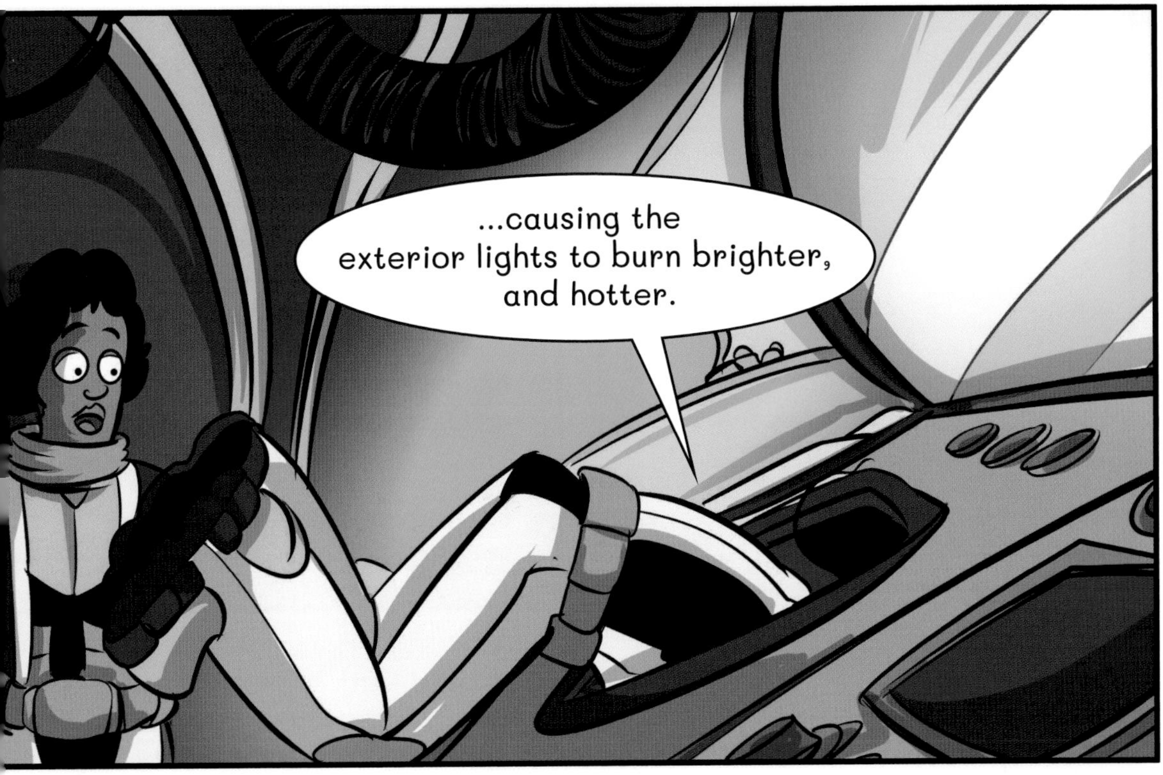
...causing the exterior lights to burn brighter, and hotter.

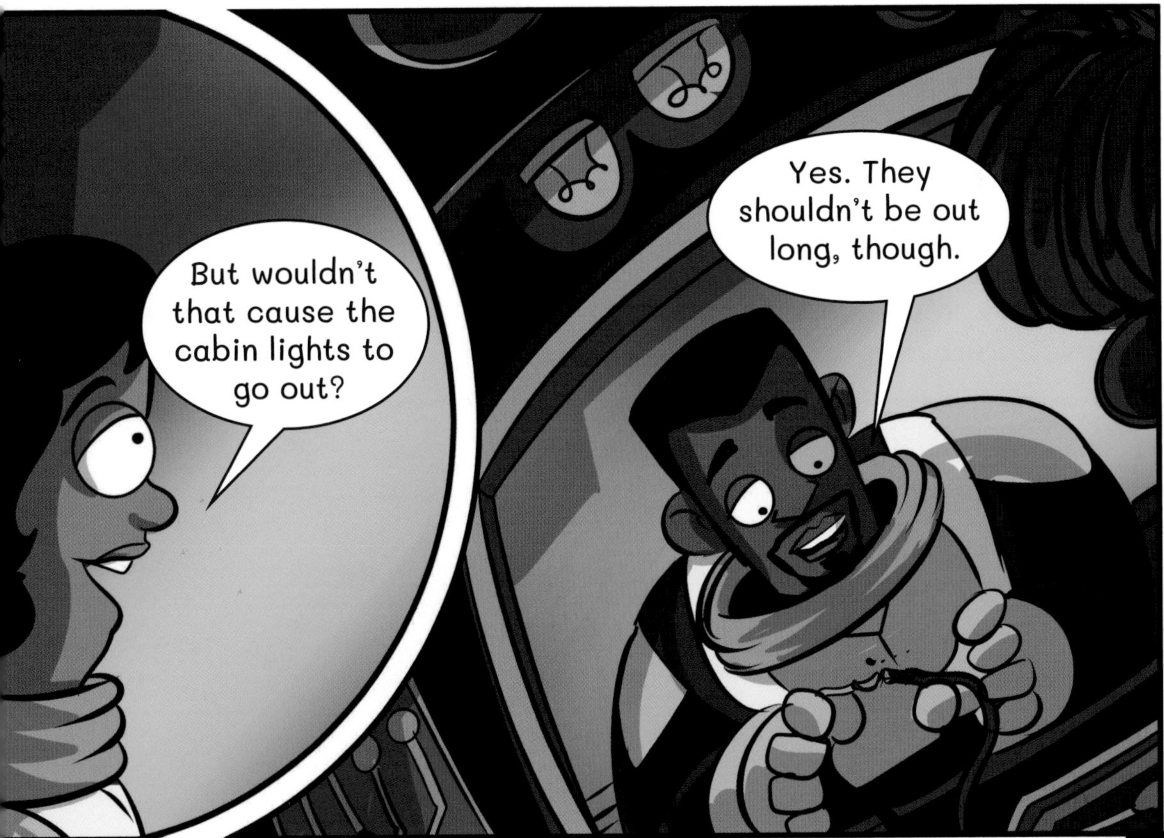
But wouldn't that cause the cabin lights to go out?
Yes. They shouldn't be out long, though.

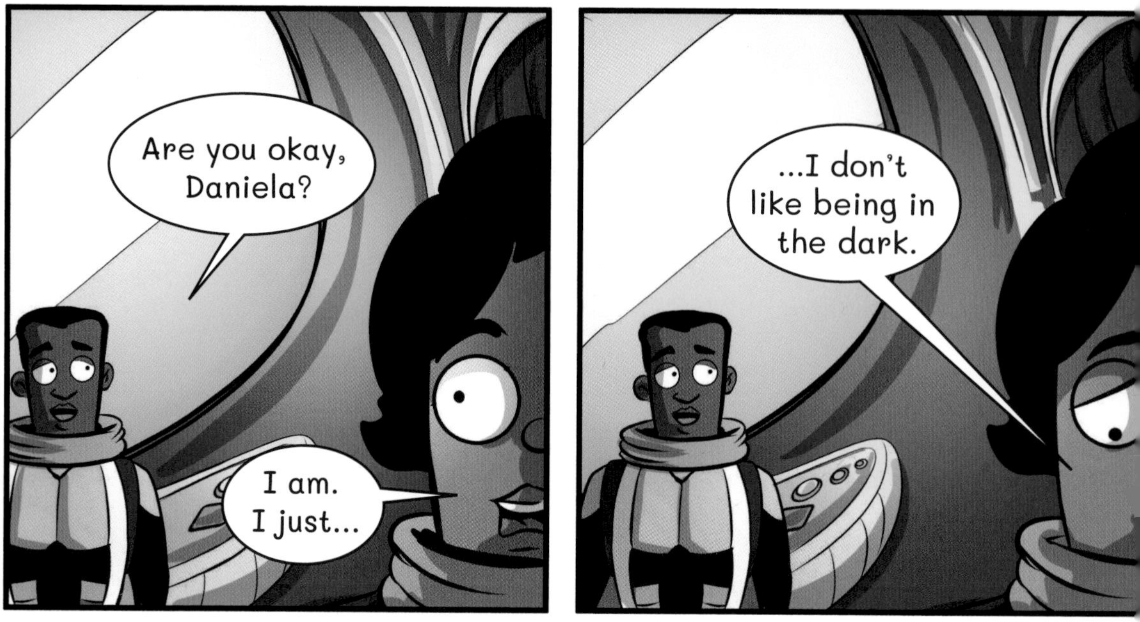
Are you okay, Daniela?
I am. I just...
...I don't like being in the dark.

SCIENCE FACT

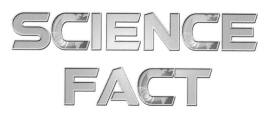

It is believed that 11 percent of the population in the United States has a fe of the dark. It is called nyctopohobia. I a good thing that Daniela does not have astrophobia. That's the fear of stars and space!

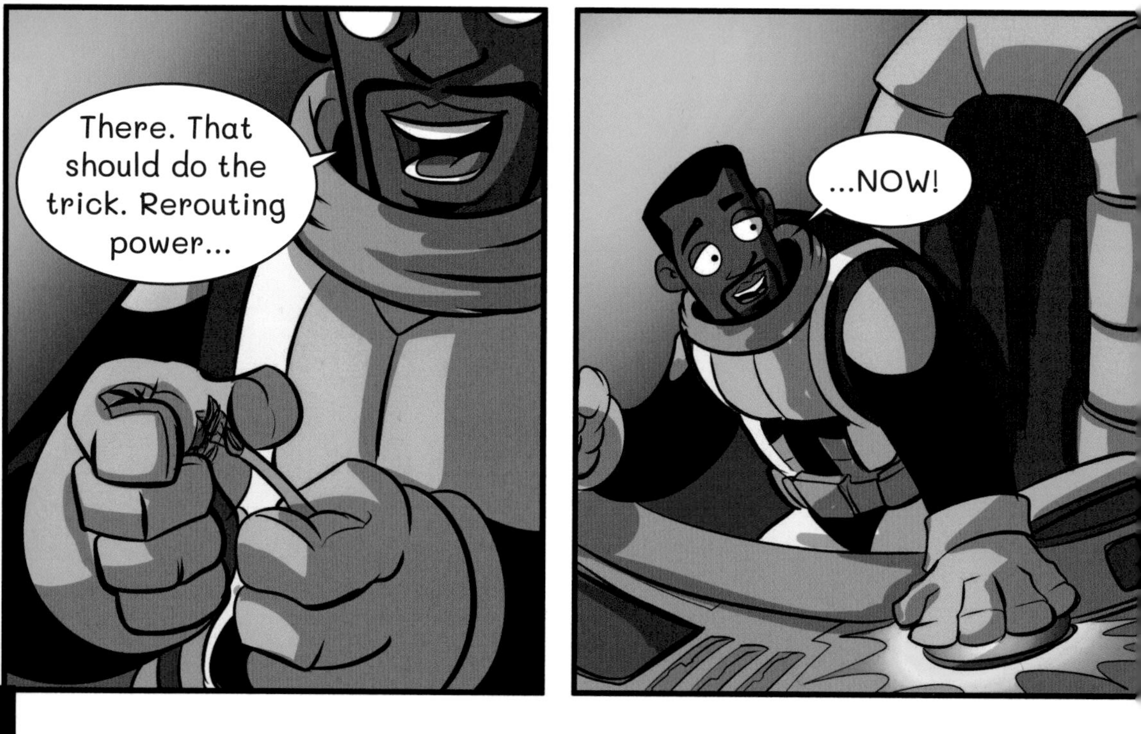
There. That should do the trick. Rerouting power...
...NOW!

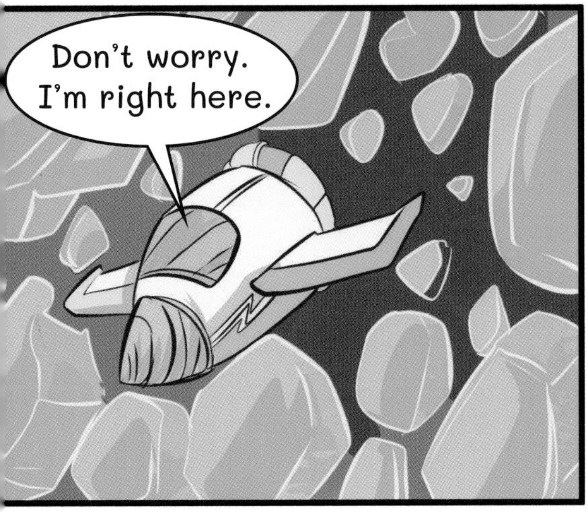
Don't worry. I'm right here.

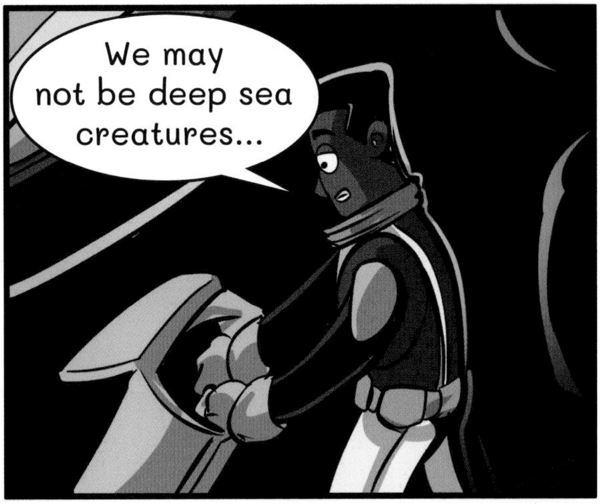
We may not be deep sea creatures...

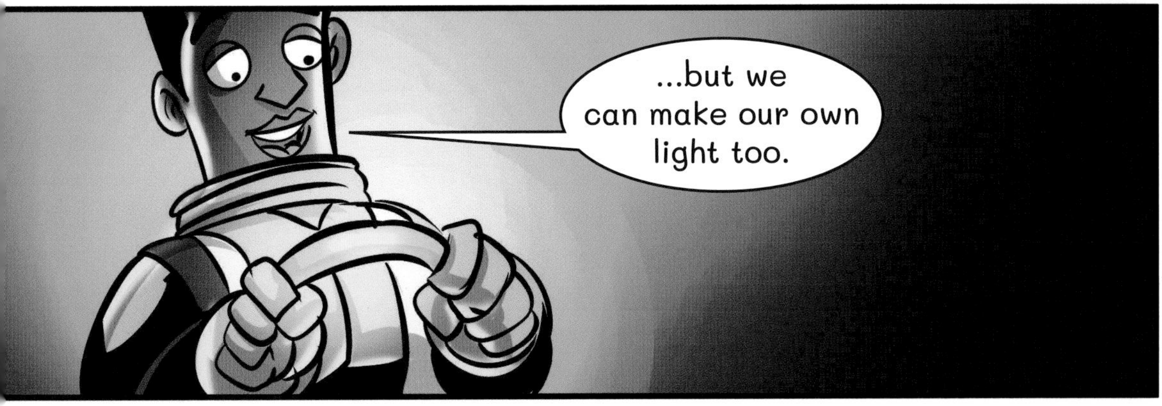
...but we can make our own light too.

SCIENCE FACT

A chemical reaction causes glow sticks to illuminate. One of the chemicals is hydrogen peroxide. In 2011, hydrogen peroxide was found in space, on grains of cosmic dust.

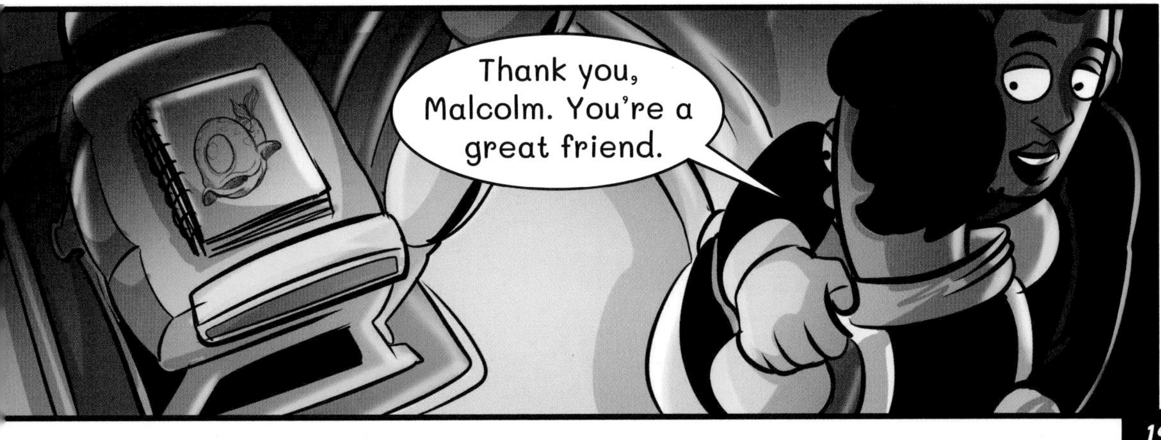
Thank you, Malcolm. You're a great friend.

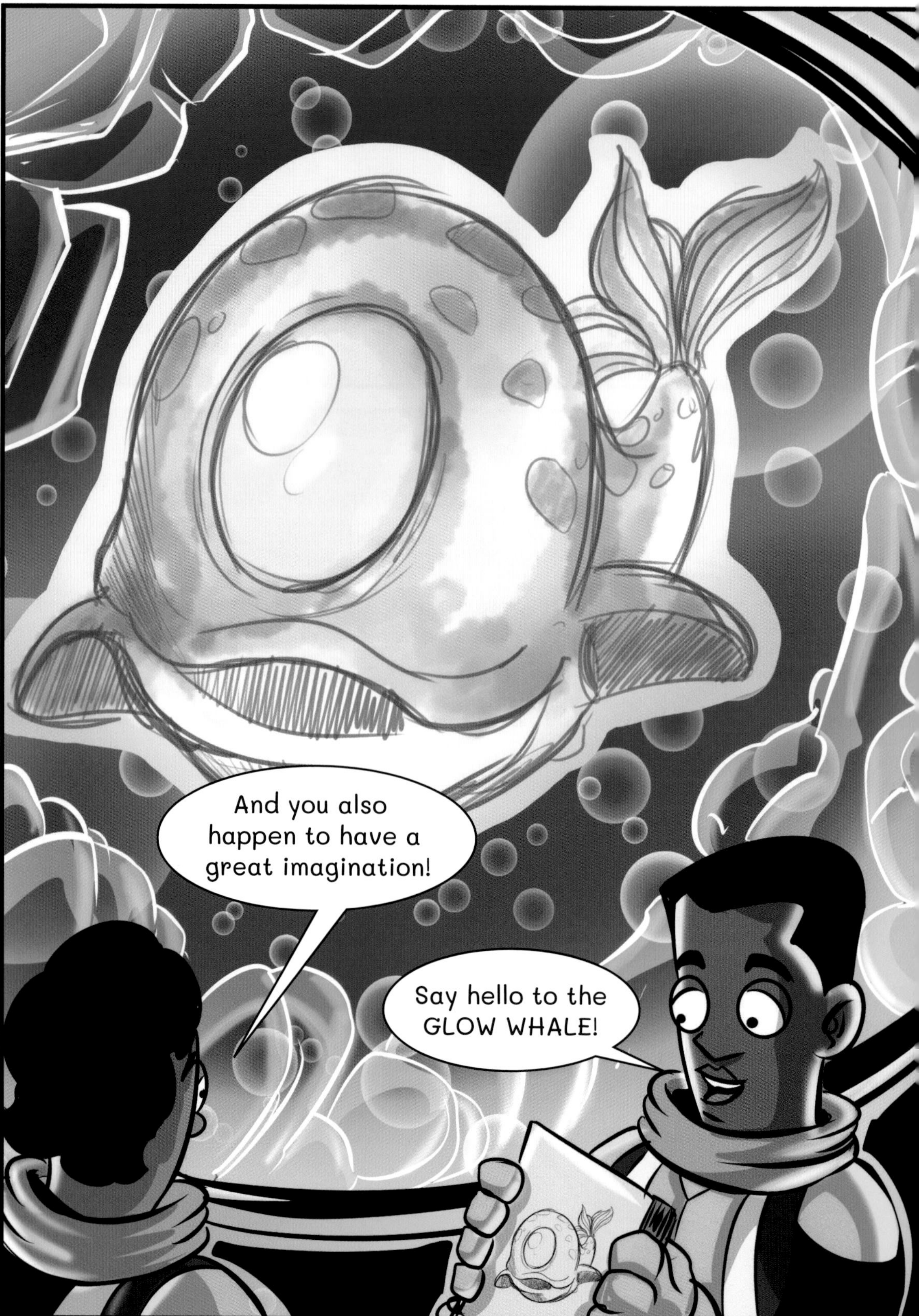
And you also happen to have a great imagination!
Say hello to the GLOW WHALE!

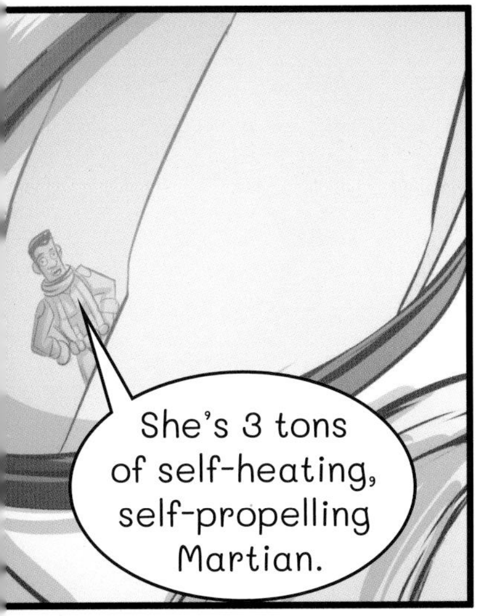
She's 3 tons of self-heating, self-propelling Martian.

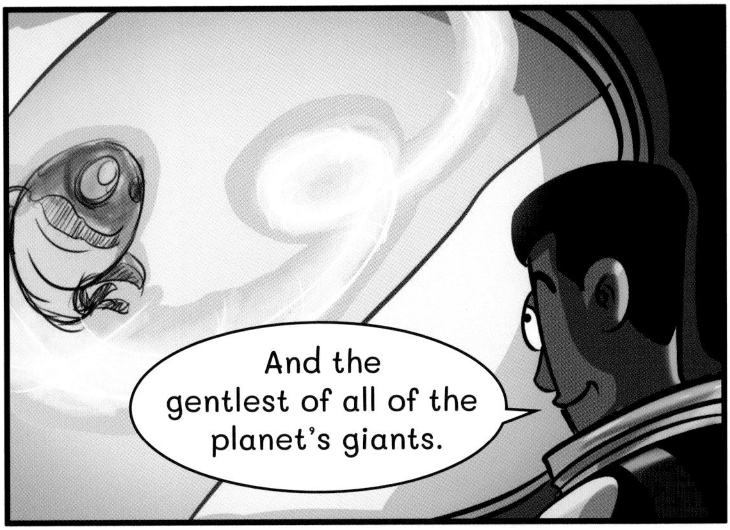
And the gentlest of all of the planet's giants.

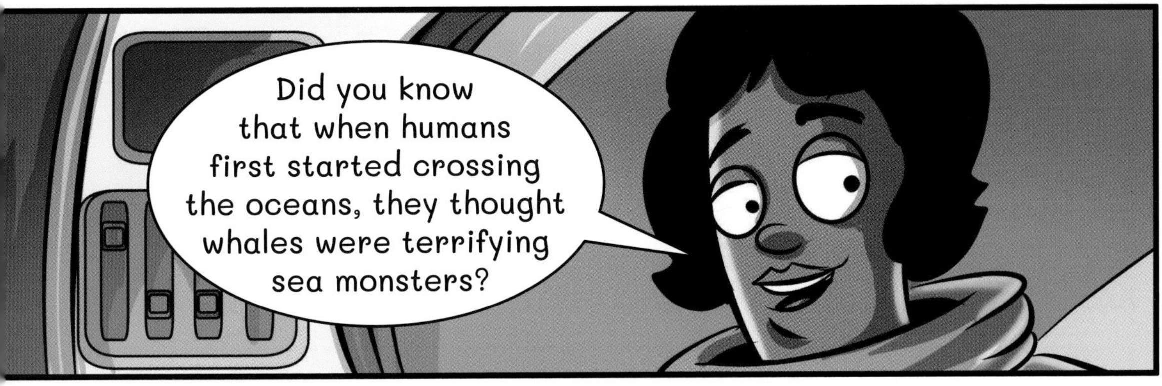
Did you know that when humans first started crossing the oceans, they thought whales were terrifying sea monsters?

SCIENCE FACT

The world record for sailing around Earth is 40 days. The fastest flight was set in 2019 by a British pilot and a NASA astronaut. It took them 46 hours, 39 minutes, and 38 seconds.

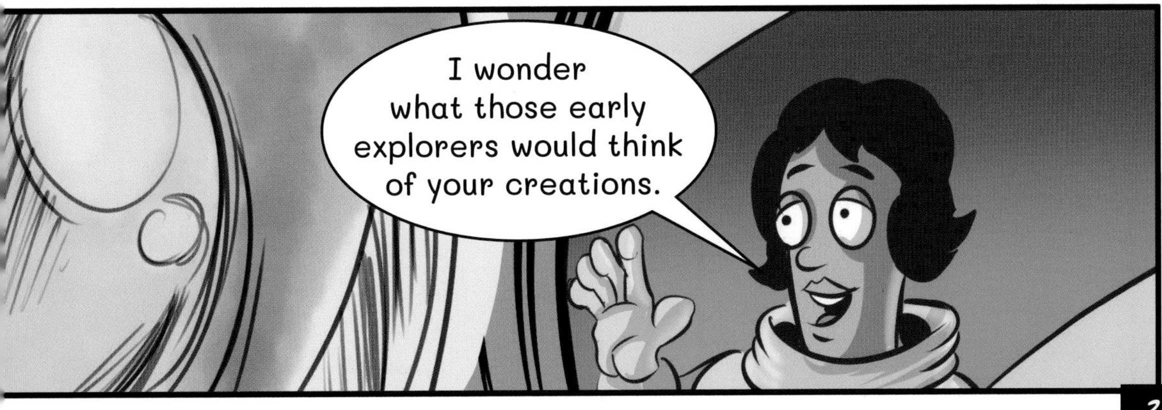
I wonder what those early explorers would think of your creations.

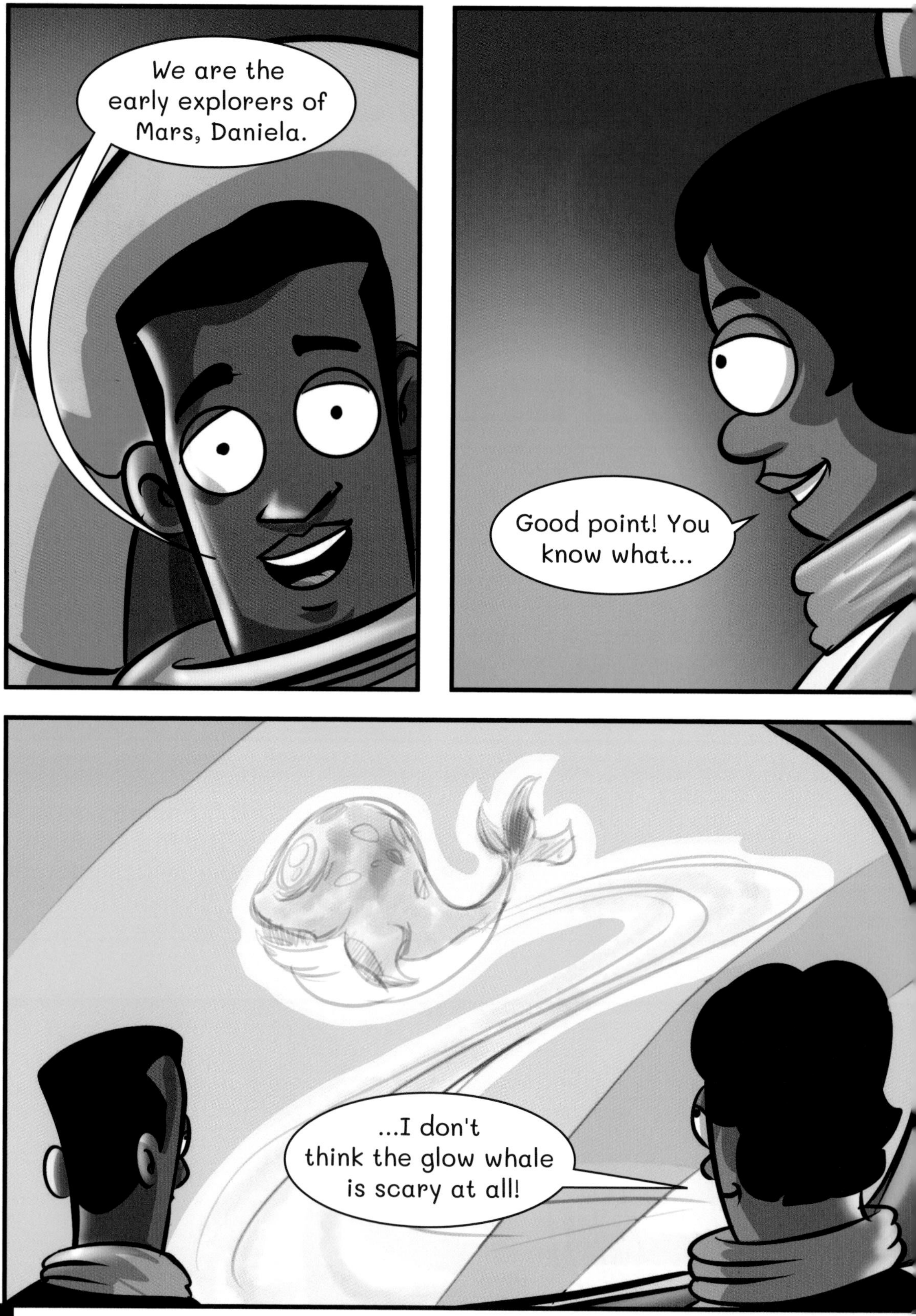
We are the early explorers of Mars, Daniela.
Good point! You know what...
...I don't think the glow whale is scary at all!

THE FUNDAMENTALS OF ART

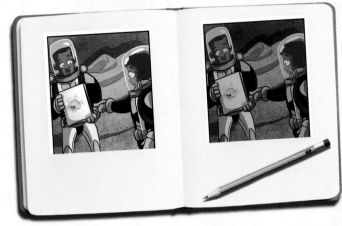

Let's put the FUN in the fundamentals of art by learning how to color an image to make it look like nighttime. Review these 2 examples of Malcolm and Daniela. Which version looks like they are standing outside during the day, and which looks like they are standing outside during the night? Let's uncover the best approach to pull this off!

• Successfully painting a night scene is all about values.

• Value means how light or dark a particular color or hue is.

• A hue is a color that hasn't been mixed. Those are the primary colors: red, yellow, and blue.

• Colors can look completely different but have the same value.

• If painting a night scene, most of the values need to be very dark or very light.

• What value you use depends on the light source. For example, is the only light in your scene coming from the Moon? The Moon does not shine as bright as the sun or a lamppost, so the values would be very dark.

ARTIST TIP: It can be dark at night but there are almost always light sources. Is there a moon in your picture? Fireflies? Or perhaps a candle? Sometimes adding a light source to your nighttime art can help make certain elements stand out.

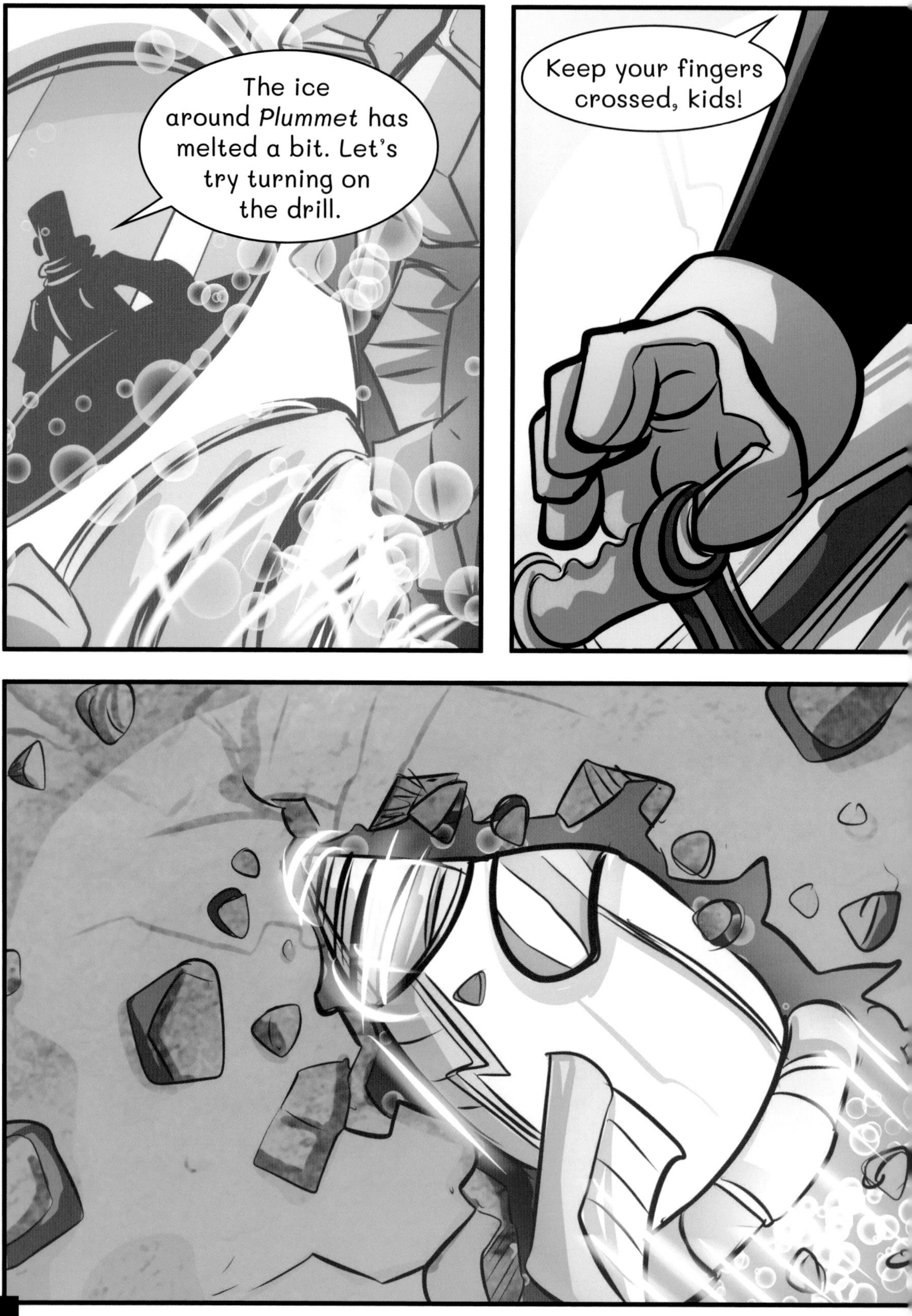
The ice around *Plummet* has melted a bit. Let's try turning on the drill.
Keep your fingers crossed, kids!

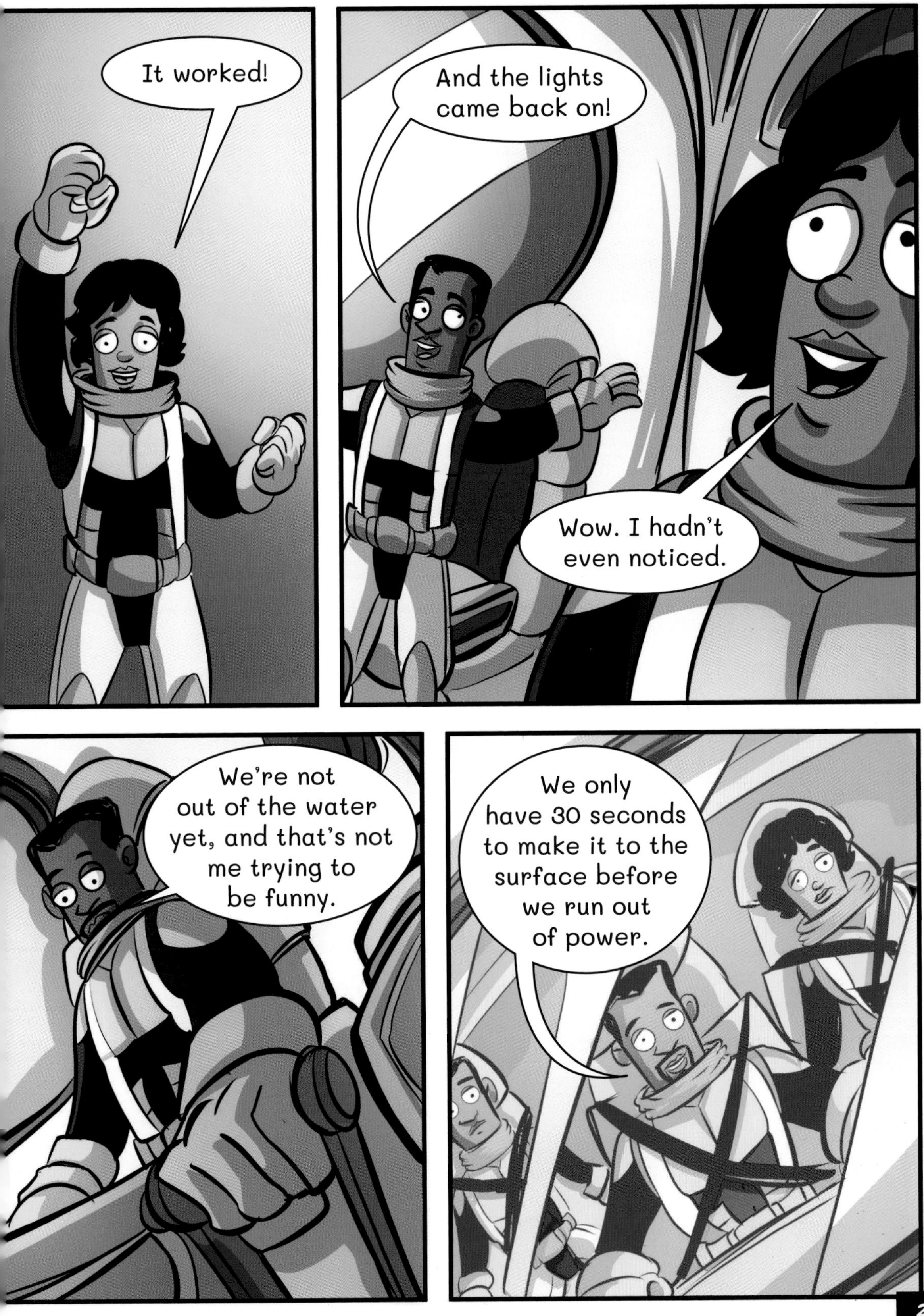
It worked!
And the lights came back on!
Wow. I hadn't even noticed.
We're not out of the water yet, and that's not me trying to be funny.
We only have 30 seconds to make it to the surface before we run out of power.

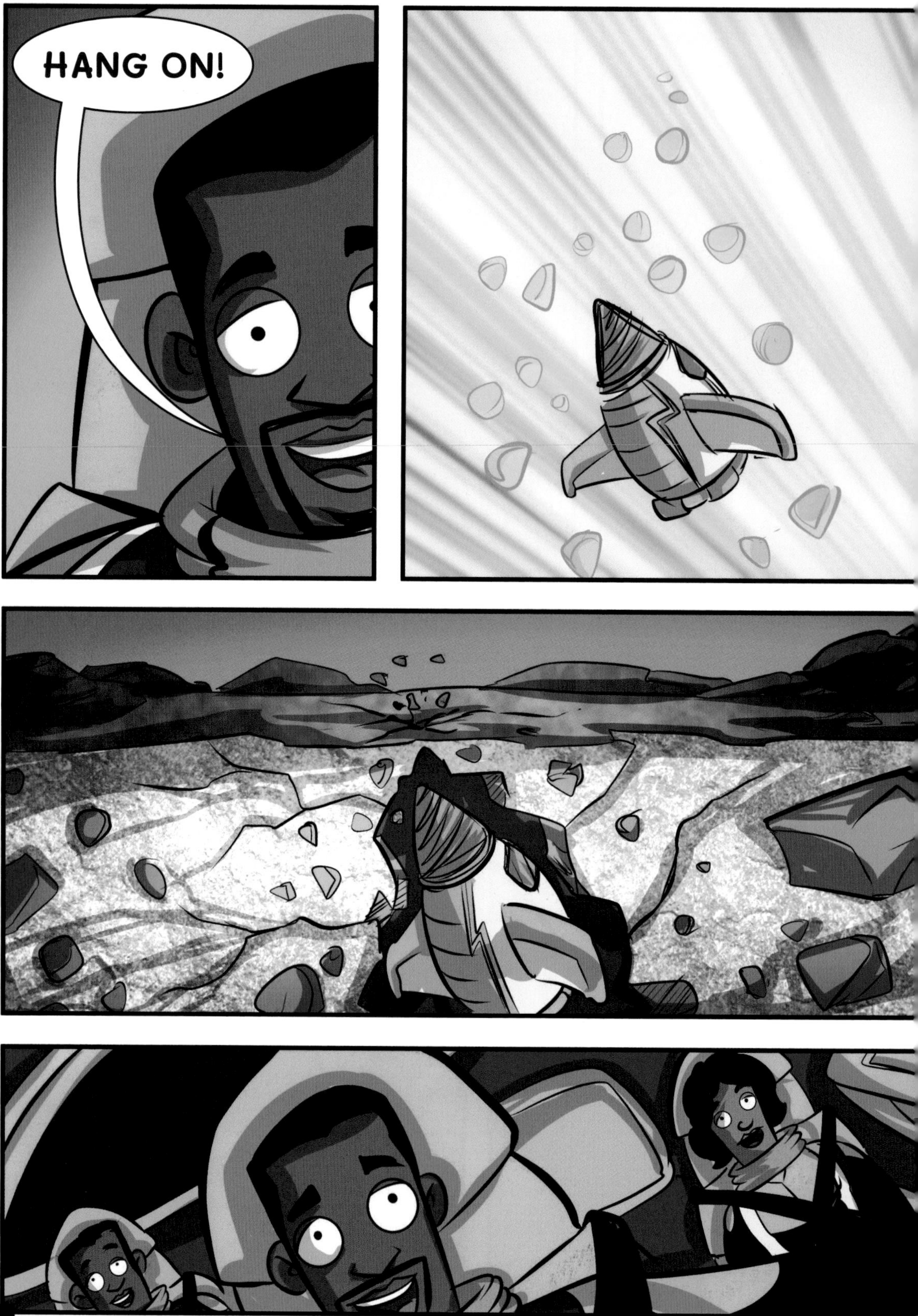
HANG ON!

MARS SURVIVAL TIPS

Surviving an unexpected cold blast is the same no matter where you are. Keep your wits and follow these tips for staying warm and dry.

• Exposed skin leads to trouble in the cold. Cover up and stay out of the wind.

• Whatever you do, do not get wet. This will cause your body temperature to drop quickly.

• If you do get wet, change your clothes immediately.

• Get your heart rate up. Jog or do jumping jacks in place. Stop before you break a sweat.

• Seek shelter. In high winds, **frostbite** can set in fast.

• The ideal temperature for the human body is 98.5°F (36.9°C). If your body temperature drops to 95°F (35°C), you are entering **hypothermia**.

• Your organs cannot operate properly in hypothermia. Your heart, lungs, brain, and kidneys will shut down.

• Signs of severe hypothermia include slurred speech, low energy, and a weak pulse. You will also stop shivering.

• If you have access to medical attention, seek it out. Hypothermia can not be reversed by covering yourself up with a blanket. You will need to have your body temperature raised through extreme measures like blood rewarming and by receiving warm fluids **intravenously**.

frostbite: the freezing of skin

hypothermia: a drop in body temperature that is dangerous

intravenously: given in a vein

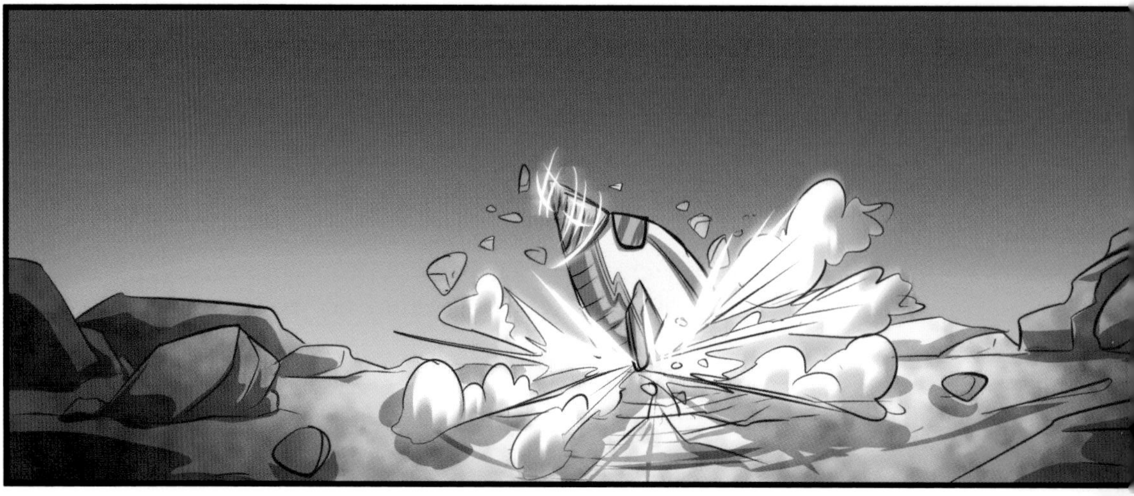

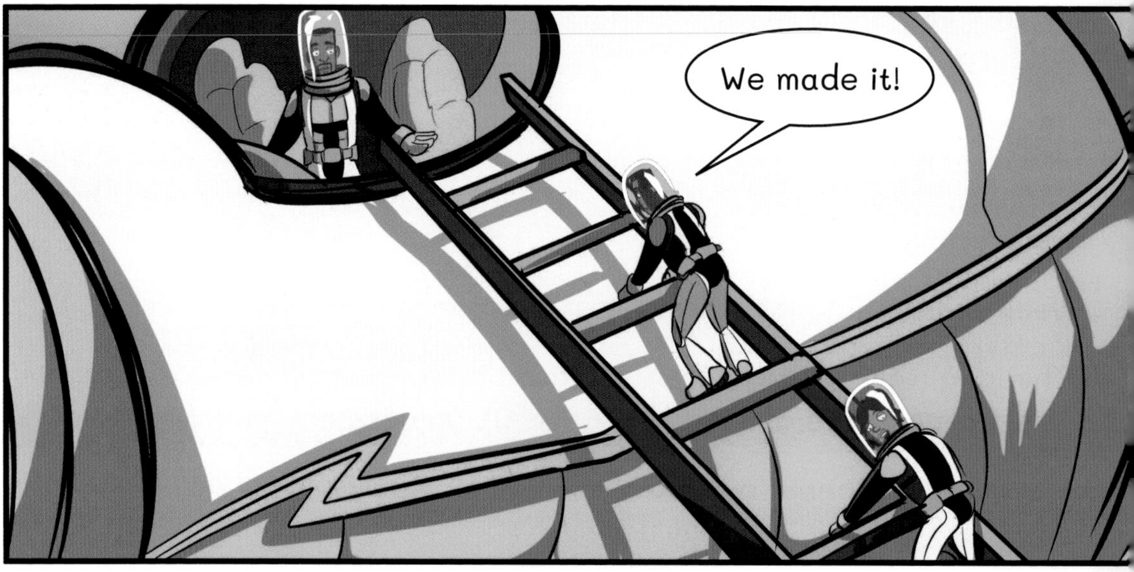
We made it!

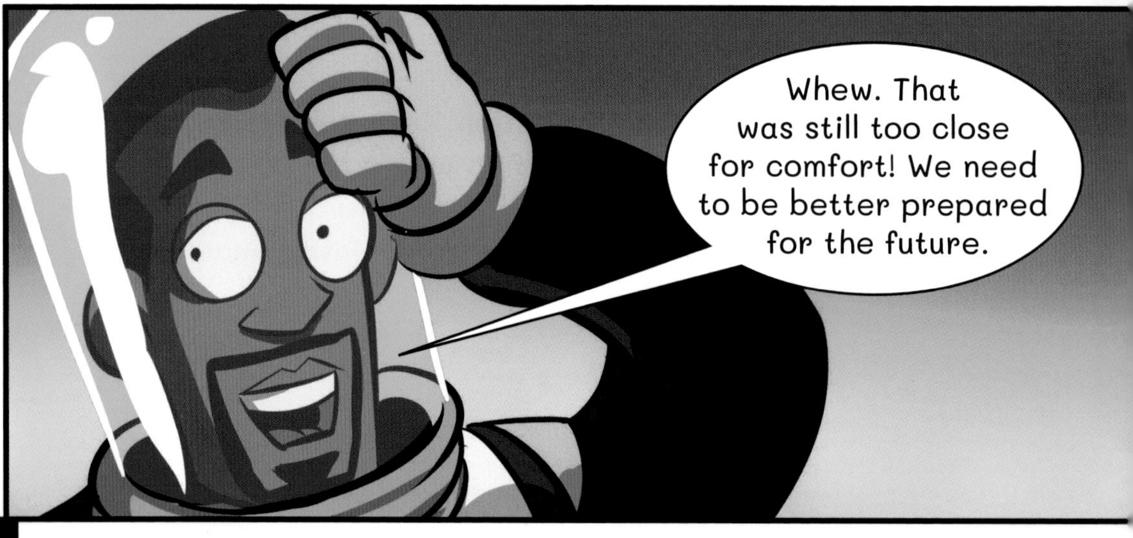
Whew. That was still too close for comfort! We need to be better prepared for the future.

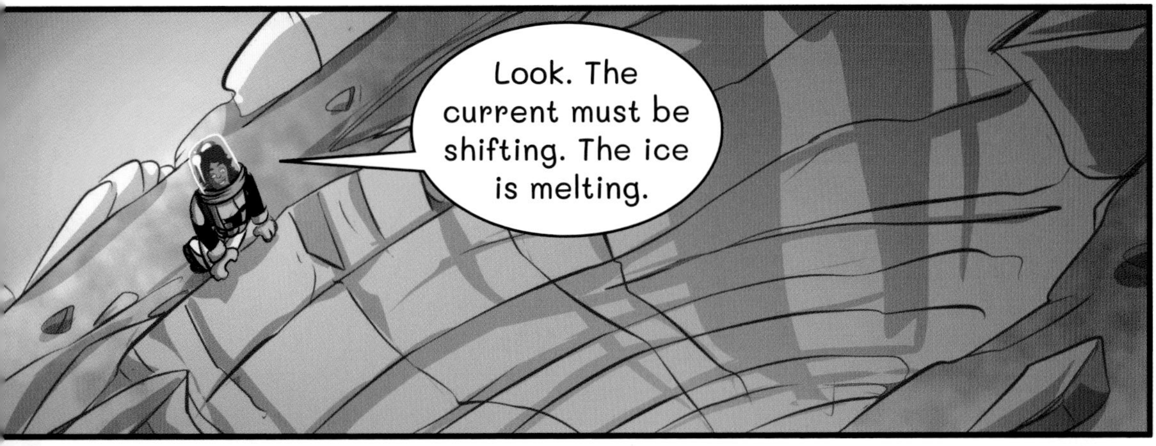
Look. The current must be shifting. The ice is melting.

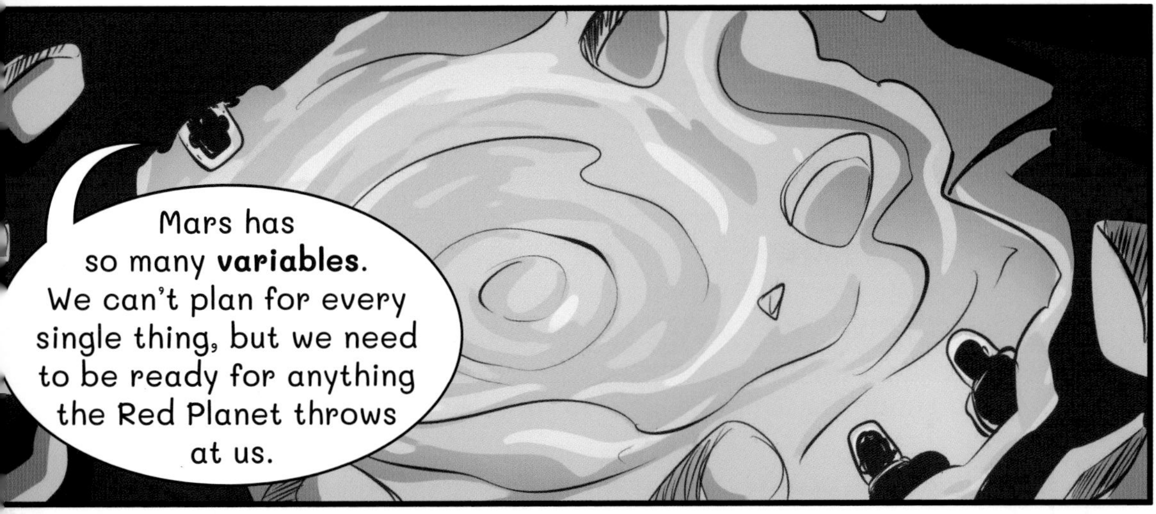
Mars has so many **variables**. We can't plan for every single thing, but we need to be ready for anything the Red Planet throws at us.

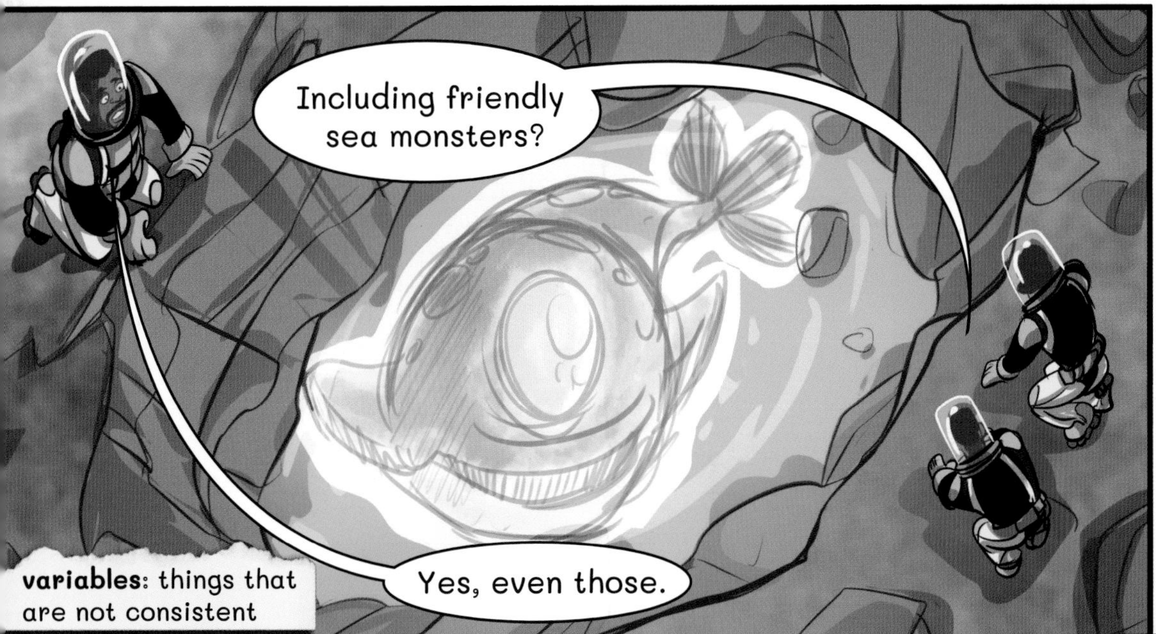
Including friendly sea monsters?
Yes, even those.

variables: things that are not consistent

FREEZE FRAME

Malcolm and the crew found themselves quickly frozen in Mars ice. Did you know that you can see water freeze in a flash while standing in your kitchen?

WHAT YOU NEED

•bottle of purified water
•freezer
•timer

STEPS TO TAKE

1. Place the bottle of water in the freezer.

2. Set a timer for 2 hours and 45 minutes.

3. Remove the bottle from the freezer. You will notice that the water still liquid, but it is very cold.

4. Now, tap the bottle firmly. The water inside the bottle will freeze right before your eyes!

LEARN MORE

BOOKS

Lonely Planet Kids. *Future Worlds*. Oakland, CA: Lonely Planet, 2021.

Vago, Mike. *The Planets are Very, Very, Very Far Away: A Journey Through the Amazing Scale of the Solar System.* New York, NY: The Experiment, 2021.

WEBSITES

Listen to NASA's Ingenuity Drone Fly on Mars
https://www.pcmag.com/news/listen-to-nasas-ingenuity-drone-fly-on-mars

What does a drone sound like on Mars? Listen and learn!

National Geographic: Why We Explore Mars
https://www.nationalgeographic.com/science/article/mars-exploration-article

Why do we explore Mars, and what have we learned?

THE MARTIANS

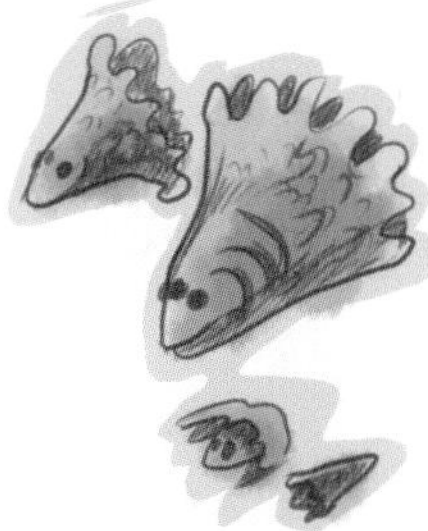

SPINY CONE FISH

Shaped like a traffic cone, Malcolm imagines this Martian lives in the underground lakes of Mars. It has luminescent scales and travels by turning itself inside out.

EMBER SQUID

Malcolm sketches this subterranean lake-dwelling Martian as it travels through the frozen water by spitting out trails of hot embers.

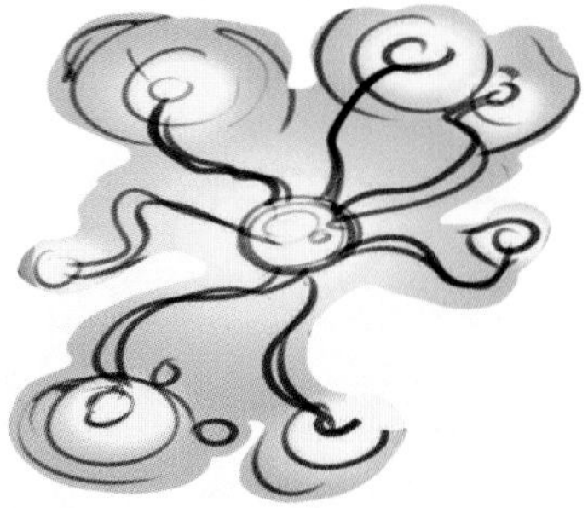

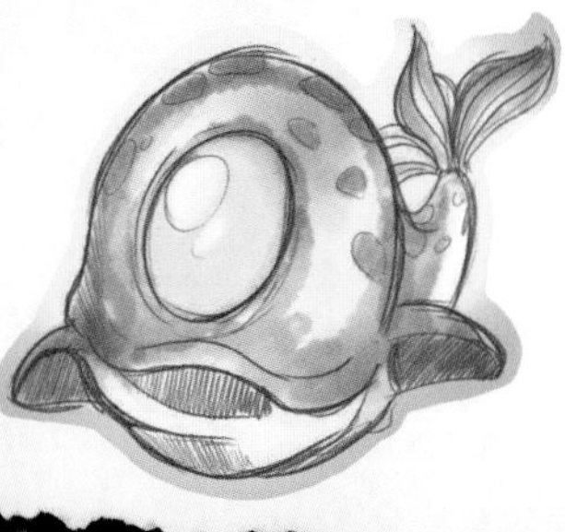

GLOW WHALES

The gentlest of all Mars giants, Malcolm draws a massive Martian that can melt the ice by forcing its body to heat and glow.

GLOSSARY

adapted (uh-DAPT-tuhd) to become adjusted to new conditions

bioluminescence (BY-oh-loo-muh-NEH-sunz) light created by a living organism

current (KUR-uhnt) continuous movement of sea water from one place to another

environment (en-VY-ruhn-mehnt) the specific place where an animal lives

formulate (FORM-yoo-layt) work up or create

frostbite (FROST-byte) the freezing of skin

hypothermia (hy-poh-THER-mee-uh) a drop in body temperature that is dangerous

insulation (in-suh-LAY-shuhn) material used to keep heat from escaping

intravenously (in-truh-VEY-nuhs-lee) given in a vein

luminescence (loo-muh-NEH-sunz) light created without a heat source

uncharted (un-CHAR-tuhd) not yet explored

variables (VEH-ree-uh-buhls) things that are not consistent

INDEX